The Picnic

The Picnic

David K. Williams

Illustrated by Laura Ovresat

Green Light Readers
Harcourt, Inc.

Orlando   Austin   New York   San Diego   Toronto   London

Todd, Kim, Mick, and Rick!

Let's go on a picnic!

Toss this, toss that—
salad for our picnic.

Pop this, pop that—
popcorn for our picnic.

Pass this, pass that.
Pack this, pack that.

Now this is a picnic!

Walk here, walk there,
on the path to our picnic.

Hop up, hop down,
on the path to our picnic.

Todd, Kim, Mick, and Rick!

Look at this big picnic!

For the Birds

The children in the story make popcorn for their picnic. You can make a popcorn snack to give to the birds!

WHAT YOU'LL NEED

wire

popcorn

dried fruit

Shape the wire into a circle.

Put popcorn and fruit on the wire.

Twist the ends together.

Hang your wreath outsid

Watch for birds to come.
Draw pictures of the birds you see.

Here Comes the Sun

Having a picnic is just one of the
things you can do on a sunny day.
What do you do when the sun is out?
Make a mural with some friends
to show "sunny day" fun.

WHAT YOU'LL NEED

mural paper   paints   brushes

1. Paint a picture to show what you do when the sun is out.

2. Tell the group about your part of the mural.

Is today a sunny day? Choose something fun from the mural to do outdoors.

Meet the Illustrator

Laura Ovresat lives in Michigan. Summer is a busy time at her house. Her kids are home from school and they always have friends over. Imagine lunchtime at Laura's house with her children and their friends making lunch. Laura did, and was inspired to paint the pictures for this story.

Requests for permission to make copies of any part of the work should be mailed to the following address: Permissions Department, Harcourt, Inc., 6277 Sea Harbor Drive, Orlando, Florida 32887-6777.

www.HarcourtBooks.com

First Green Light Readers edition 2006

Green Light Readers is a trademark of Harcourt, Inc., registered in the United States of America and/or other jurisdictions.

Library of Congress Cataloging-In-Publication Data
Williams, David K.
The picnic/by David K. Williams; illustrated by Laura Ovresat.
p.   cm.
"Green Light Readers."
Summary: Four friends enjoy a picnic together.
[1. Picnicking—Fiction.   2. Stories in rhyme.]
I. Ovresat, Laura, ill.   II. Title.   III. Series: Green Light reader.
PZ8.3.W6735Pic   2006
[E]—dc22   2005013115
ISBN-13: 978-0152-05776-3   ISBN-10: 0-15-205776-5
ISBN-13: 978-0152-05782-4 (pb)   ISBN-10: 0-15-205782-X (pb)

A C E G H F D B
A C E G H F D B (pb)

Ages 4-6
Grade: 1
Guided Reading Level: D-E
Reading Recovery Level: 4-5

Green Light Readers
For the reader who's ready to GO!

"A must-have for any family with a beginning reader."—*Boston Sunday Herald*

"You can't go wrong with adding several copies of these terrific books to your beginning-to-read collection."—*School Library Journal*

"A winner for the beginner."—*Booklist*

Five Tips to Help Your Child Become a Great Reader

1. Get involved. Reading aloud to and with your child is just as important as encouraging your child to read independently.

2. Be curious. Ask questions about what your child is reading.

3. Make reading fun. Allow your child to pick books on subjects that interest her or him.

4. Words are everywhere—not just in books. Practice reading signs, packages, and cereal boxes with your child.

5. Set a good example. Make sure your child sees YOU reading.

Why Green Light Readers Is the Best Series for Your New Reader

- Created exclusively for beginning readers by some of the biggest and brightest names in children's books

- Reinforces the reading skills your child is learning in school

- Encourages children to read—and finish—books by themselves

- Offers extra enrichment through fun, age-appropriate activities unique to each story

- Incorporates characteristics of the Reading Recovery program used by educators

- Developed with Harcourt School Publishers and credentialed educational consultants